First U.S. edition 2006

Library of Congress Cataloging-in-Publication Data is available.

Library of Congress Catalog Card Number pending

ISBN-10 0-7636-3183-3   ISBN-13 978-0-7636-3183-3

Printed in Singapore   10 9 8 7 6 5 4 3 2 1

This book was hand-lettered by Jez Alborough.   The illustrations were done in gouache on board.

Candlewick Press   2067 Massachusetts Avenue, Cambridge, Massachusetts 02140

visit us at www.candlewick.com

YES

Jez Alborough

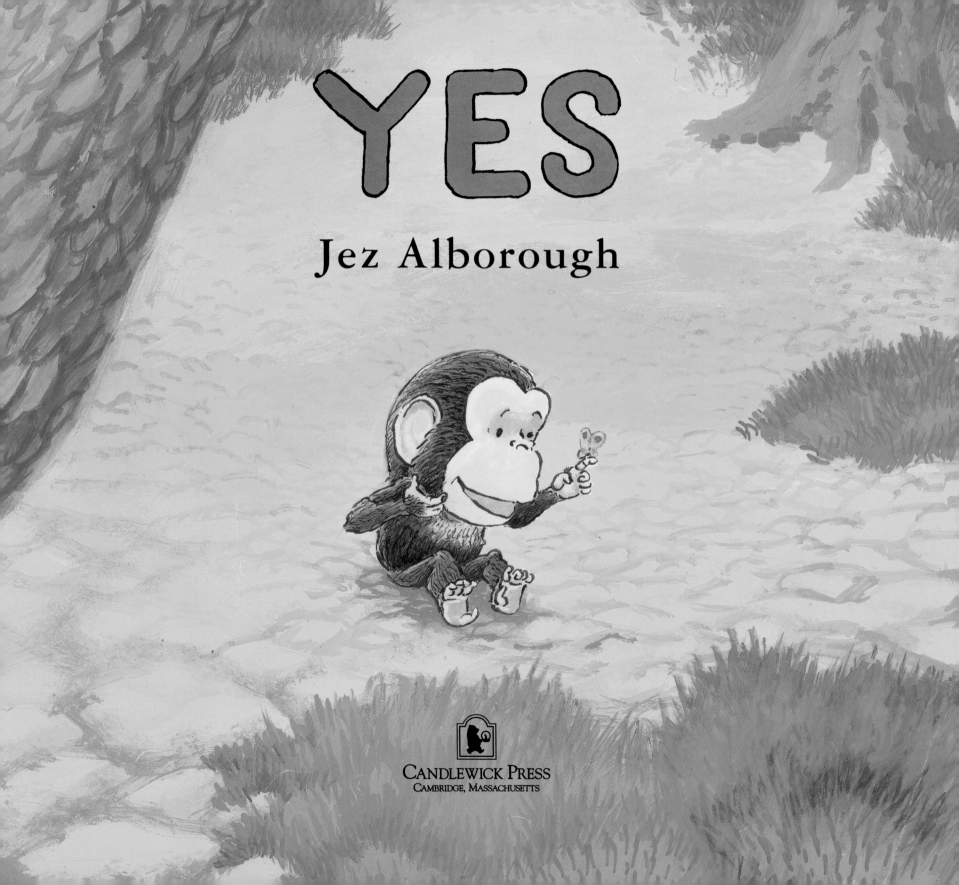

CANDLEWICK PRESS

CAMBRIDGE, MASSACHUSETTS